An I Can Read Book®

A PURPLE CRAYON ADVENTURE

A Picture for Harold's Room

by CROCKETT JOHNSON

HarperCollins*Publishers*

A Picture for Harold's Room
Copyright © 1960 by Crockett Johnson
Copyright renewed 1988 by Ruth Krauss Johnson
For information address HarperCollins Children's Books, a division
of HarperCollins Publishers, 10 East 53rd Street, New York, NY
10022.

Library of Congress Catalog Card Number: 60-6372
ISBN 0-06-023005-3
ISBN 0-06-023006-1 (lib. bdg.)
ISBN 0-06-444085-0 (pbk.)

14 15 16 SCP 10

A Picture for
Harold's Room

"I want a picture to put

on my wall," said Harold.

He drew a house with

his purple crayon.

More houses made a little town.

It was far away.

The town had woods and
hills around it.

And it was at the end of

a long road.

"It will look pretty in the
moonlight," said Harold.

And he stepped up into the
picture to draw the moon.

He looked down at the houses.

"I am a GIANT!" he said.

But a giant would scare

all the people in town.

"It is good no one woke up
and saw me," said Harold.

He walked over the hills.

"How big I am!" he said.

Harold's head was above

the clouds.

With a few steps he came

to the end of the land.

And at the end of any land

there is water.

"It is the sea," said Harold.

"There are sea gulls."

19

Harold was big enough to
walk through the sea.

A great big ship went by.

It was an ocean liner.

A big whale came up in the
waves, spouting water.

And just ahead of Harold

was an old sailing ship.

He easily caught up with
it and passed it.

The sea ended against a
steep hill.

Harold needed some rocks

to step on.

He climbed out of the sea
and onto the hill.

Then he saw that the ship
was too near the rocks.

He put up a lighthouse

to show the sailors.

And he went on his way

over high mountains.

Harold was taller than
the highest mountain.

"I am higher than anything!"

he said.

Then, suddenly, he thought
of airplanes.

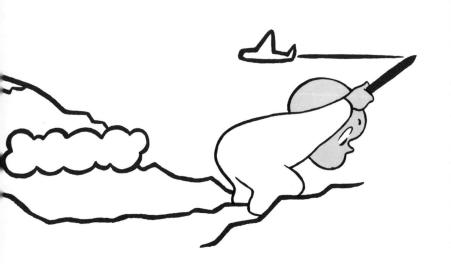

Harold ducked his head

just in time.

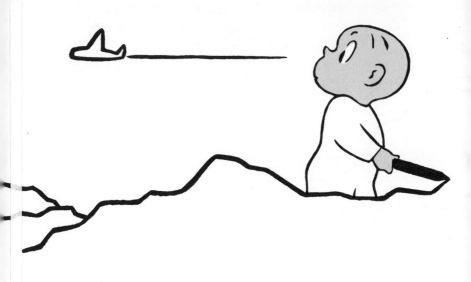

It was a big jet plane,

flying very fast.

There might have been

a bad accident.

Harold found a low place

in the mountains.

It was a good place for a
railroad to go through.

It came out onto a long
flat field.

Harold put some birds and
flowers near the tracks.

"People like to see things

from trains," he said.

He went on, drawing tracks

and birds and flowers.

And he had to keep looking
out for trains.

It was a big job for

a small boy.

44

And all of a sudden he saw

how small he had become.

He was half the size

of a daisy!

He was smaller than a bird!

How would he get home?

He could not wade home
through the ocean.

He could not climb

those high mountains.

And, just then, he fell

into a mouse hole.

"Excuse me," he said

to the mouse.

Then Harold sat down

on a pebble to think.

After a minute or two

he stood up again.

"This is only a picture!"

he said.

And he took his crayon

and he crossed it out.

"I am not big or little.

I am my usual size!"

But how could he be sure

about that?

At home he was always

his usual size.

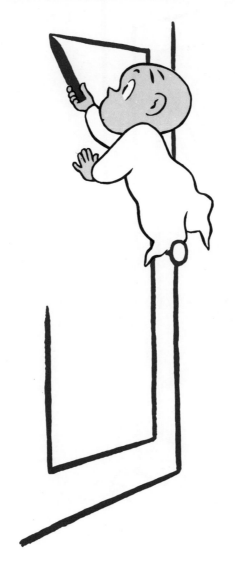

So he drew the door

of his room.

There was a long mirror

on the back of the door.

"Yes," said Harold.

"I am my usual size."

He was glad to be back

in his room. He was tired.

But he had no picture
to hang on his wall.

So, before he went to bed,

he drew another picture.